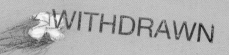

For B. P-H. and my gorgeous Tom, Rafi & Gabriel,
YOU make me happy —S. P-H. x x x x

For JB, and for best friends big and small xx —A. B.

BLOOMSBURY CHILDREN'S BOOKS
Bloomsbury Publishing Inc., part of Bloomsbury Publishing Plc
1385 Broadway, New York, NY 10018

BLOOMSBURY, BLOOMSBURY CHILDREN'S BOOKS, and the Diana logo
are trademarks of Bloomsbury Publishing Plc

First published in Great Britain in January 2019 by Bloomsbury Publishing Plc
Published in the United States of America in January 2019
by Bloomsbury Children's Books

Bloomsbury books may be purchased for business or promotional use. For information on bulk purchases please contact
Macmillan Corporate and Premium Sales Department at specialmarkets@macmillan.com

Library of Congress Cataloging-in-Publication Data
available upon request
ISBN 978-1-68119-849-1 (hardcover)
ISBN 978-1-5476-0171-4 (e-book) • ISBN 978-1-5476-0172-1 (e-PDF)

Art created with acrylic paint and colored pencil
Typeset in Birka
Book design by Kristina Coates
Printed in the U.S.A. by Worzalla, Stevens Point, Wisconsin
4 6 8 10 9 7 5 3

All papers used by Bloomsbury Publishing Plc are natural, recyclable products made from wood grown in well-managed forests.
The manufacturing processes conform to the environmental regulations of the country of origin.

To find out more about our authors and books visit www.bloomsbury.com and sign up for our newsletters.

You Make Me Happy

Smriti Prasadam-Halls   illustrated by Alison Brown

BLOOMSBURY
CHILDREN'S BOOKS

NEW YORK   LONDON   OXFORD   NEW DELHI   SYDNEY

You make me happy,
you make me sing.

There's a bounce in my footstep,
like bunnies in spring.

You make me happy,
like birds taking flight,

like a waterfall twinkling,
like morning's first light.

The things that you do, and the things that you say,
fill me with sunshine and brighten my day.

You're so full of wonder.
I'm full of surprise.

We see things afresh
through each other's eyes.

You show me the fun
in whatever we find.

We know we look silly . . .
but hey, we don't mind!

You love to be cheeky, you know that you do . . .

. . . but I can't seem to *ever* stay grumpy with you.

Whenever you hug me, so tight and so sweet,
my toes start to tingle, my heart skips a beat.

When the going gets tough and life makes me frown,
when my heart starts to sink like the sun going down . . .

you bring back the sunshine and, out of the blue,
you make me laugh with the things that you do.

I find that I'm giggling, I find that I'm glad,
I find that I'm smiling, no time to be sad.

And when I look into
your bright, sparkly eyes,
there's a song in my heart,
there are stars in the skies.

You make me happy,
you make me new.
Together there's NOTHING
that we cannot do.

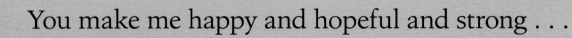

You make me happy and hopeful and strong . . .

. . . and right by your side
is where I belong.

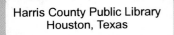